Franny K. Stein

MAD SCIENTIST

FRANTASTIC VOYAGE

FRANTASTIC VOYAGE

JIM BENTON

ALADDIN PAPERBACKS

NEW YORK   LONDON   TORONTO   SYDNEY

For
Griffin, Summer, Mary K, and
all the other monsters I've met along the way

ACKNOWLEDGMENTS

Editors: Joanna Feliz and Kevin Lewis
Designer: Lucy Ruth Cummins
Art Director: Dan Potash
Production Editor: Katrina Groover
Managing Editor: Dorothy Gribbin
Production Manager: Chava Wolin
Associate Paperback Editor: Molly McGuire

❧

ALADDIN PAPERBACKS
An imprint of Simon & Schuster Children's Publishing Division
1230 Avenue of the Americas, New York, NY 10020
Copyright © 2005 by Jim Benton
All rights reserved, including the right of reproduction in whole or in part in any form.
ALADDIN PAPERBACKS and colophon are trademarks of Simon & Schuster, Inc.
Also available in a Simon & Schuster Books for Young Readers hardcover edition.
The text of this book was set in Captain Kidd.
Manufactured in the United States of America
First Aladdin Paperbacks edition May 2006
18 20 19 17
The Cataloging-in-Publication Data is on file with the Library of Congress.
ISBN-13: 978-1-4169-0229-4 (hc.)
ISBN-10: 1-4169-0229-5 (hc.)
ISBN-13: 978-1-4169-0230-0 (pbk.)
ISBN-10: 1-4169-0230-9 (pbk.)

0712 OFF

CONTENTS

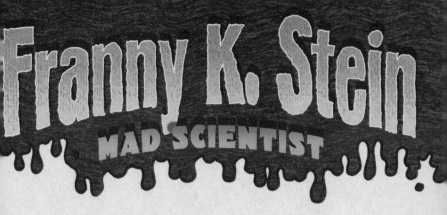

FRANTASTIC VOYAGE

CHAPTER ONE

FRANNY'S HOUSE

The Stein family lived in the pretty pink house with lovely purple shutters down at the end of Daffodil Street. Everything about the house was bright and cheery. Everything, that is, except the upstairs bedroom with the tiny round window.

Behind this window was Franny's room, which was also her laboratory.

Even for a mad scientist, Franny's lab was unusual. Her experiments and inventions were far beyond those of your average, everyday mad scientist.

In fact Franny's work was so complicated that she found she could not do it alone. She had a lab assistant named Igor.

Well, he wasn't a *pure* lab. He was also part poodle, part Chihuahua, part beagle, part spaniel, part shepherd, and possibly part some kind of weasly thing that probably wasn't even a dog.

Franny had been through a lot with Igor, and he had learned a great deal about mad science working with Franny in her laboratory.

But Igor was still awfully young and Franny was still nervous about letting him work on any of the more dangerous projects.

CHAPTER TWO
FRANNY LOSES FACE

Franny remembered the time that she was working on a device that would make bite-size jelly doughnuts with the press of a button, but Igor got the dimensions wrong and she wound up filling the entire school with jelly.

Then there was that time Franny was try-ing to create a beautiful new kind of striped flower by adding the DNA from a tiger to an ordinary houseplant. But Igor read the plans wrong and the two of them were nearly eaten by a bouquet.

And she could never forget when she invented the Automatic Face Scrubber. Igor changed one of the settings and it pulled Franny's face right off.

Luckily Franny was pretty good at emergency surgery and managed to get her face reattached without too much trouble.

Igor could be a real pest sometimes, and Franny's upcoming project was going to be so dangerous that she just could not risk Igor messing things up.

Franny knew that there were people who handled pests every day; pests like scorpions, termites, and the very worst of all:

her brother.

CHAPTER THREE
MOM KNOWS PEST

Franny could sneak a rabid warthog into the house without anybody hearing it.

She could raise a family of electric eels in the toilet without ever getting shocked.

She could even make a cloned *T. rex* ride a unicycle.

But she could not handle her brother, Freddy.

Franny noticed that Freddy never really bothered her mom.

She could cook, and read, and change the oil in the car, and Freddy never seemed to be in her way.

Franny just knew that if she tried to do any of those things, both Freddy and Igor would bug her like crazy.

Franny wondered what sort of brilliant methods her mom was using to restrain Freddy.

PERHAPS SHE SUSPENDS HIM OVER A TANK OF BRAT-EATING PENGUINS,

OR ENCASES HIM IN A BLOCK OF ICE. (THIS WOULD ALSO CONTROL THE ODOR)

SHE MIGHT
BE USING
MUMMIFICATION,

OR PICKLING,

OR MAYBE SHE
HIDES AUNT EDNA'S
GLASSES AND
TELLS HER THAT
FREDDY IS A
SMALL, UGLY CHAIR.

But Franny's mom had used an even simpler, more effective, and more diabolical restraining device than Franny could ever have imagined. With just the press of a button, this gadget kept Freddy totally out of her way while she worked.

CHAPTER FOUR

TUBE HEAD

Franny's mom pressed a button on the remote control and the television came on. Freddy stopped in mid-step and slumped down on the floor in front of it.

Franny was fascinated. Freddy was trans-
fixed by the screen. "It's like he's hypnotized,"
she said.

She waved her hand in front of his face and
he did nothing.

Franny left and came back with a few things from her lab.

She waved a black widow spider, a vampire bat, and a cobra in front of his face, and still he did nothing but stare at the TV.

Franny began to grin. "This may be what I need," she said. And after looking through a book about electronics, she assembled a TV and remote control for her dog.

Franny set up the new television in front of Igor. "I know that there's nothing you like better than helping me with my work, Igor," she said softly. "But give this a look and see if you might be willing to watch it once in a while when I need to work alone."

Franny pressed the button on the remote control and the TV came on. Igor slumped down on the floor and stared at it.

She waved tarantulas, bones, and even a small monster she had recently made in front of Igor, and all he did was stare at the screen.

"Perfect," said Franny. "This is perfect."

CHAPTER FIVE
DOGGY SEE, DOGGY DO

Okay, maybe it wasn't exactly perfect. The TV kept Igor occupied, but it seemed to have another strange effect on him.

If he saw a commercial for bubble gum, he'd start chewing some right away.

If he saw a show about boats, he'd pretend to be a sailor.

If he saw a movie about a king, he'd start behaving like one.

He wanted all the things he saw on TV, even if he had no idea why he would ever want them.

Once he saw a commercial for soda fifteen times in the same day and he drank so much that his burps kept Franny and everything else in the lab awake all night.

Franny knew that the TV was the real problem, but it kept Igor out of the way, so she decided to just make a No Burping rule, and let him keep watching it.

At least she'd let him watch it until she completed the Doomsday Device.

CHAPTER SIX

HAPPY DOOMSDAY TO YOU

Over the last year or so Franny had begun to realize that the things in her lab could do terrible things if they ever fell into the wrong hands.

She worried about some evil secret government department stealing her Permanent Wave Machine and threatening everybody on Earth with incredibly dumb-looking hairdos.

Or what if a cruel alien life-form got a hold of her design for the Piranha Trike? Piranha could overrun the world in no time.

And she imagined that an evil mad scientist could discover her plans for Remote-Control Underpants. With this technology he could give the entire world a gigantic mass wedgie.

So, in order to protect humanity from these and countless other creations, she completed her work on the Doomsday Device.

Even though it was not much bigger than a gumball, it was probably the single most powerful explosive ever created.

If it ever looked like her technology was about to fall into the wrong hands, Franny could set the timer on the device and blow up her lab, protecting the world from all of her inventions.

What would be left of the world, anyway.

CHAPTER SEVEN

THAT'S A LITTLE TOUGH TO SWALLOW

Franny had put in a long day completing the Doomsday Device and she was sleeping very soundly, dreaming the kind of dream that mad scientists always seem to dream.

Suddenly Igor, who was in a terrible panic about something, shook Franny awake. He had drawn spaceships shooting lasers and written the words "alien invasion" on a piece of paper. He waggled it at Franny and pointed frantically toward the sky.

Franny, still groggy, staggered to her feet
and stumbled to the special safe where she
kept the Doomsday Device.

"It's a good thing I completed it in time," she
said. "I'll just set it down here in case we need to
use it." She placed the device on the table and
went to her telescope.

Franny scanned the sky. "I don't see them yet," she said. "I wonder if they're planning some sort of a sneak attack."

She looked over at Igor, who was sitting on a chair, watching TV, and snacking on grapes.

Her eyes narrowed. "Igor, you certainly look calm for somebody who is expecting an alien invasion." Igor did not look up from the television.

Franny looked back up at the sky. There were no spaceships, no laser beams, and no aliens.

"Igor, where exactly did you see the aliens coming to invade the Earth?"

Igor pointed at the TV.

It was a movie about aliens invading Earth.

Franny was stunned for a moment. "A movie?" she said.

Igor looked up from the TV this time.

"You saw it in a movie?" Franny began to shout. "A movie?! Do you have any idea the danger you put us all in because you saw some people in rubber alien costumes? I was even getting ready to activate the Doomsday De—" Franny stopped yelling in mid-sentence.

She pointed at the table. "Where's the
Doomsday Device? I set it on the table, right
there next to your plate of grapes."

Igor shrugged his shoulders and tried to smile the kind of smile you smile when you know you've done something wrong, but you're hoping that nobody can tell. Franny knew that smile. She had used it herself many times.

Franny grabbed Igor and set him down in front of her X-ray machine. She could see the Doomsday Device in his stomach.

"I knew it! You ate it! You couldn't even take your eyes off the TV long enough to make sure that you were eating a grape and not a bomb!"

She quickly pulled her stethoscope from a drawer and listened to his stomach. She heard it ticking.

"You activated it! You must have bitten down on the button and started the timer!

"I don't know how to tell you this, exactly, Igor. But let's just say that in less than an hour, it might be raining kibble all over the world."

CHAPTER EIGHT

IGOR, YOU DA BOMB

Franny had to think fast. You really don't have that many options when your dog swallows a horrifically devastating explosive and you only have sixty minutes to act. Ask anybody who's been in that situation. They'll tell you the same thing.

Franny made some notes and considered the various choices.

I COULD PUT IGOR IN A ROCKET AND SHOOT HIM TO THE MOON

BUT THE BLAST WOULD DESTROY THE MOON

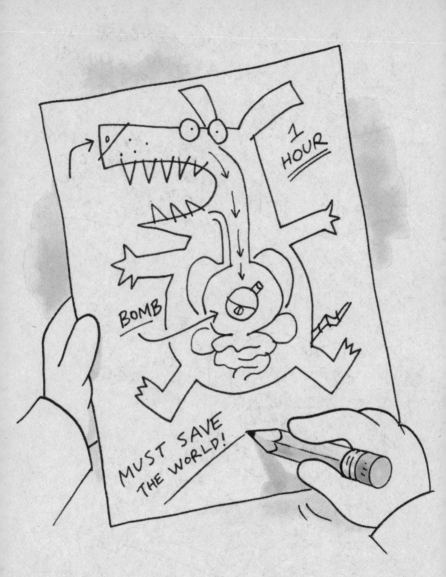

"There's really only one conclusion.
I'm going in."

CHAPTER NINE

SNOT SOMETHING YOU WANT TO DO

Franny began putting on a special suit. "This will protect me from the various horrible juices inside a dog."

Igor scowled.

"No hard feelings, Igor. But if you think you stink on the outside, take a whiff of one of your disgusting dog burps sometime. This is a fantastically unbelievable voyage I'm going on, but it's no pleasure cruise in there."

Igor smelled his own breath. He had to agree with Franny: He was probably even worse on the inside.

"Here's my plan. First I'll use my Shrinkerizer to miniaturize myself. Then I want you to carefully sniff me right up your nose."

Igor pointed at his mouth.

"No. Not your mouth. I'm going in through your nose. I can't trust those teeth of yours. You could accidentally bite me in half."

Franny pointed at a chart of Igor's body.

"Once inside your nose, I'll make my way down your throat to your stomach."

Igor handed her a flashlight.

"Good thinking, Igor, but my suit is glow-in-the-dark, and that will light my way.

"When I get to your stomach, I'll find the device, open it up, and deactivate it. This screwdriver is all I'll need.

"Now, about getting back out," Franny began. Igor looked a little nervous.

"After I find the device and deactivate it, I'll call you on this walkie-talkie. Then you just lie down on your stomach, and that will make it easy for me to roll the device out like a big ball. I'll just walk right back out your nose."

Igor nodded in agreement.

"Then I'll reverse the Shrinkerizer with this remote control, enlarge to my normal size, and everything will be back just fine.

"I'll also be able to watch you on this little screen on my wrist, just to make sure you're okay throughout the procedure. You can even sit here and watch your dumb TV while you wait."

Igor clapped his little paws together.

Franny checked her watch. There were less than forty-five minutes left. "Everything seems to be in order," she said. "What could go wrong?"

Chapter Ten
LOOKING UP AN OLD FRIEND

Franny pressed a button and stood in front of the Shrinkerizer. Igor watched as she shrank down to almost nothing.

Igor gently crept up and positioned his nose
carefully. Franny looked up his giant nose and
braced herself. With one giant snort, she was
sucked up inside his tremendous nostril.

Some people in her situation might get the willies. Some people might get the creeps. Some people might run home, jump in the bathtub, and never, ever, ever stop washing. But Franny didn't really mind walking around inside a dog's nose.

It's kind of like a cave, she thought. *A big slippery, boogery cave.*

Her feet made sloppy squishy sounds as she trotted along, and she thought about how she might actually have had fun in there, if she had more time.

CHAPTER ELEVEN
LET'S GET THE SINUS BEHIN' US

Franny stood at the edge of Igor's sinuses, looking down into his deep, dark throat. It was important that she went down his esophagus or she could wind up in one of his lungs.

She checked the screen on her wrist and saw
Igor staring at the television. A bomb was about
to go off in his stomach, and a little girl was
walking around up his nose, and he couldn't care
about anything but the show he was watching. "I never should have given him that TV,"
Franny said.

Franny backed up a few steps to get a running start. She hurled herself off the edge and tumbled down Igor's throat. It was a much longer fall than she had expected, and she realized that it was going to be a very long walk back out.

Eventually she landed with a thick, mucky splash in his stomach.

Looking around, all she could think about
was how truly lovely the inside of a dog's nose
is when compared to the inside of his stomach.

CHAPTER TWELVE
YOUR STOMACH IS BOTHERING ME

The contents of Igor's stomach were truly a disgusting spectacle to behold. As Franny floated around on a wad of doughnut, she saw grapes, pizza chunks, and bites of hot dog churning around in a sea of partially digested gunk. Stalactites of dog food dripped gravy onto the bits of chew toy and clumps of hair that bobbed around in the swirling currents of gobbled-up food.

Franny could see all sorts of odd things that Igor had swallowed, including what was probably part of a shoelace, and the tiny foot off a plastic doll.

She couldn't see the Doomsday Device anywhere. She thought it might be below the surface.

"Last one in is a rotten egg," she said, just as a rotten egg floated past.

She checked her watch again and jumped in.

CHAPTER THIRTEEN

I THINK I GOT GUM IN MY HAIR. AND EVERYWHERE ELSE.

Franny was running out of time. If she didn't find the device quickly, that would be the end of her and Igor, and her lab, and a gigantic chunk of planet Earth.

Franny thought, *Sometimes I wonder if I should just stop building these sorts of horribly destructive things in the first place.*

Franny laughed a little. "Yeah, right," she said.

And then she spotted it, the Doomsday Device, bobbing next to a piece of peanut brittle. It had floated up to the surface and was ticking down the seconds until it would explode.

Franny swam toward it as fast as she could, paying no attention to the peculiar pink strands that swayed between her and the bomb.

Just as she was about to grab the device, Franny found she could go no farther. She looked down and saw that her legs were tangled in the sticky pink junk. She tried to free herself and got her hands stuck in it as well. The more she struggled, the worse she became entangled.

"Gum!" Franny said. "That dog has been swallowing his bubble gum!"

Franny had been so close, but now it looked like it was over. She was completely trapped by the gum, and time was running out.

"Wait a second," she said, and she wiggled her way over to the peanut brittle. "These edges are almost like broken glass!" She rubbed the strands of gum up and down the edge of the peanut brittle and began cutting and slicing until she was free.

She grabbed the Doomsday Device and pulled out her screwdriver. "You can't stop a mad scientist with a little gum," she said.

CHAPTER FOURTEEN

BUT YOU CAN STOP ONE WITH A LITTLE SCREWDRIVER

Franny smiled confidently. She hadn't expected the gum, but everything else was going according to plan.

"All I have to do now is slip this teeny little screwdriver into this great big screw and then I can open the bomb and turn it off.

"Great *big* screw? Teeny *little* screwdriver?"
Franny gasped. "Gadzooks! I miscalculated! The
screwdriver is too small to open this screw. I
can't get the device open before it explodes!"

Franny looked around Igor's stomach. "If
only there were something in here I could use."
But Igor hadn't swallowed a screwdriver.

Yet.

"The walkie-talkie!" Franny said. "I'll just tell Igor to swallow a screwdriver!"

She looked at her watch again. "But I've got to hurry. We're running out of time!"

Franny pushed the button on the walkie-talkie. "Igor! Can you hear me? Igor."

She looked at the small screen on her wrist. Igor was not responding. He just kept staring at the television.

"Igor! Can you hear me?"

Franny looked at the tiny screwdriver again and she realized the second miscalculation she had made.

"My mouth, my vocal chords, my voice! They all got smaller. Of course Igor can't hear me. My teensy voice is just too soft now!"

Franny sat down on a lump of what may have once been a pancake—gooey, yes, but actually kind of comfy.

"Let's see now. Trapped in dog stomach. No way to radio for help. Bomb going off any minute. Even if Igor were to lie down on his own, I still could never roll the bomb out in time.

"Think, Franny, think."

CHAPTER FIFTEEN

CHANNEL SURFING

Franny looked at her equipment. She had a screwdriver, her watch, and the remote control for the Shrinkerizer.

"Yeah, the remote control," she said, suddenly grinning broadly. She quickly unscrewed the back and started making some adjustments.

"I made Igor's TV and its remote control. I should be able to rewire this one so that I can control the TV from here!"

Franny looked at her wrist screen and pushed a button on the rewired remote control. She could see the channel change on Igor's television.

"Success!" she shouted. "Now watch carefully, you little tube head," she said.

Franny started switching channels feverishly. She could see the channels fly past Igor's gaze.

She passed commercials for cars, toys, blue jeans, and hamburgers.

"C'mon, c'mon, c'mon!" she yelled. "Trying to save the world here!"

Finally she stopped on a commercial for corn chips.

"This is what I need," she said.

Igor watched the commercial for a minute
and then Franny saw him leave the room. In a
moment he was back with a bag of corn chips.

"I knew he'd want them!" Franny said.

Franny saw fragments of munched-up corn chips start tumbling into Igor's stomach. "Perfect, exactly what I need," she said, grabbing two triangular bits and pulling them to one side.

"Now hopefully all the corn chips have made him thirsty."

Franny watched Igor on her little screen. He
may have been thirsty, but he wasn't going
anywhere.

Franny could hear the Doomsday Device
ticking down.

"Oh, come on, Igor. Who doesn't get thirsty
from corn chips?" she yelled.

"I think he needs a little inspiration," she said, and started changing the channel again.

She found a broadcast of a marathon with tired, hot runners racing down a scorching road. "This should make him thirstier," she said. And Igor ran out of the room.

He returned a moment later wearing running shoes and a number on his chest.

"No, no, no!" Franny yelled. And she changed the channels until she found a movie about some people lost in the desert.

"Look how thirsty they look! This will get to him."

Igor ran out of the room and returned with sunscreen and a map of the desert.

"No! No! No!" Franny yelled, and she changed the channels until she found a science show about the sun.

"The surface of the sun is over ten thousand degrees Fahrenheit," the narrator explained.

"This should do it," Franny said, and watched as Igor ran out of the room.

He returned a moment later with a glass of juice.

"No! No! No!" Franny shouted. "Juice won't work!" She started clicking through the channels feverishly.

The fate of the world depended on Igor not drinking the juice.

Just then she found what she was looking for. "Yes!" Franny shouted.

Igor stopped with the glass just inches from his mouth to have a look at the root-beer commercial Franny had switched to.

Igor watched the kids pouring the sparkling cold root beer into tall glasses. His eyes widened while they enjoyed big gulps of the delicious icy soda. He started to drool in his lap as they licked the delicious foam from their lips. He couldn't stand it anymore. He ran from the room.

He returned a moment later with a can of root beer. He plopped down on the floor and began drinking greedily.

Fizzy root beer started pouring into Igor's stomach. "Yahoo!" Franny yelled. "Success!"

CHAPTER SIXTEEN
AGAINST GASTRONOMICAL ODDS

Franny started sticking her corn chips together with clumps of gum.

The bubbles in the root beer were increasing the pressure in Igor's stomach.

She checked her watch. They were running out of time.

"Okay, Igor, let's have one of your big, disgusting burps," she said.

But Igor didn't burp. The pressure was building in his stomach, but he wouldn't burp.

Franny remembered what she had told him. "Gadzooks," she said. "Igor is trying to follow my rule. He's keeping himself from burping."

NO BURPING

Franny started changing channels. "We'll
see about that, Igor," she said.

She found a music video with an irresistible
beat.

Igor started tapping his foot.

Franny popped the back off her remote and
made a few little adjustments. Now she could
control the volume of Igor's TV, and she made
the music louder.

Igor's shoulders started to move a little in time to the music.

Franny turned up the music a little more.

Igor's tail started to sway back and forth.

Franny howled, "For the love of all humanity, shake what your mama gave you!"

Franny increased the volume as loud as it

would go and Igor finally lost control.

He bopped, grooved, and danced just like the people in the music video.

His dancing was working on his stomach the way that shaking works on a bottle of root beer.

"He can't hold this burp back forever," Franny said.

As the pressure grew, Franny made the final adjustments to her corn chips, and stuck the Doomsday Device in place with more gum. She began her countdown: "5-4-3-2-1..."

Igor couldn't hold it back any longer. The pressure in his stomach was just too great, and he burped a huge, gassy dog burp.

"Blastoff!" Franny yelled. She had built a Windsurfer out of the corn chips and held it tightly as she rode the root-beer burp straight up Igor's throat.

She rocketed right out of his mouth, moving much too fast to worry about his snaggly teeth, and skidded to a complete stop right in front of the Shrinkerizer.

She fumbled with the wires in the remote. She was starting to panic. Only a minute remained until the bomb went off.

"Calm down, Franny," she said to herself.

She got the wires back in their original positions. She hit the button and enlarged to her regular size. She grabbed the Doomsday Device, opened it up with the screwdriver, which was now the correct size, and with only two seconds before it exploded, she managed to turn it off.

Igor, Franny, her lab, and half the world
were saved.

She turned to Igor. "It's okay now, Igor.
We're safe."

Igor smiled.

"But I have to ask you: Why did you eat a doll's foot?"

Igor shrugged. *Seemed like a good idea at the time,* he thought.

CHAPTER SEVENTEEN

A WEAPON OF MASS AFFECTION

Franny wasted no time dismantling the Doomsday Device. "That might have been the worst thing I ever made," she said.

Then she turned her attention to the TV she had built for Igor. "And this might be the second worst."

Igor jumped in front of the TV. He knew
Franny was about to smash it to bits.

"Stand aside, Igor. This thing has to go," she
said, and she began selecting an appropriate
smasher from her collection.

Igor knew begging wouldn't help. Then he
noticed the remote control.

Franny chose a weighty battle-ax that had been useful in the past when other experiments had gone badly and had required swift disassembly.

Igor frantically clicked through the channels.

Franny raised the battle-ax. Igor kept switching, kept switching, kept switching until finally...

Franny froze in mid-swing. It was a science show about spiders.

The narrator said, "A single black widow spider can have more than twenty-five hundred babies a year."

"Awww! Wook at the widdle babies," she gushed, dropping the ax and settling into Igor's chair.

Igor smiled broadly and cuddled up next to her.

"I know what you're thinking, Igor," she said. "You're thinking that shows like this will persuade me to keep the TV."

Igor smiled and nodded.

"Well, let me think. It's true that the TV caused a lot of trouble, but I guess I was the one who made the Doomsday Device in the first place and without the television, we would've been blown to bits."

"Okay, we'll keep it. But you have to promise me a few things."

Igor clapped.

"You can only watch it once in a while. There are lots of other things to do around here."

Igor nodded.

"You have to try not to let it make you think that you want things. Commercials can be very tricky that way."

Igor wagged his finger at the TV.

"And one more thing," Franny said.

"You must never, ever, ever stop burping."

Igor took a long drink of his root beer and let a huge burp fly.

Franny laughed and the two of them cuddled up in Igor's chair and watched 2,500 adorable newborn babies eat a mountain of flies.